THE QUEEN'S HAT

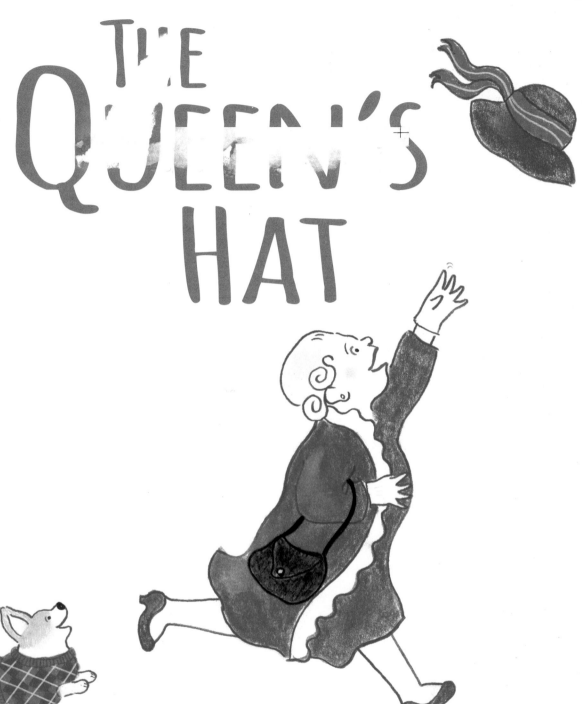

For Mum, Dad and Joseph.
Without you, this book wouldn't exist.

First published in hardback in 2014 by Hodder Children's Books
This edition published in 2014

Hodder Children's Books, 338 Euston Road, London, NW1 3BH
Hodder Children's Books Australia, Level 17/207 Kent Street,
Sydney, NSW 2000

A catalogue record of this book is available from the British Library.

ISBN 978 1 444 91915 8

Printed in China

Hodder Children's Books is a division
of Hachette Children's Books,
an Hachette UK Company

www.hachette.co.uk

THE QUEEN'S HAT

Steve Antony

h

*Hodder
Children's
Books*

A division of Hachette Children's Books

The Queen was
on her way to
visit someone very
special when the
wind went...

swish!

The wind took the Queen's favourite hat right off her head.

It soared high above the Queen.
It wooshed high above the Queen's men.

The wind was so strong that it
swept the Queen's hat all the way to...

Trafalgar Square...

and all through...

London Zoo...

and all along...

the London Underground...

and all around...

the London Eye...

and all across...

Tower Bridge...

and all over...

Big Ben....

where it sailed up further into the sky...

swooosh!

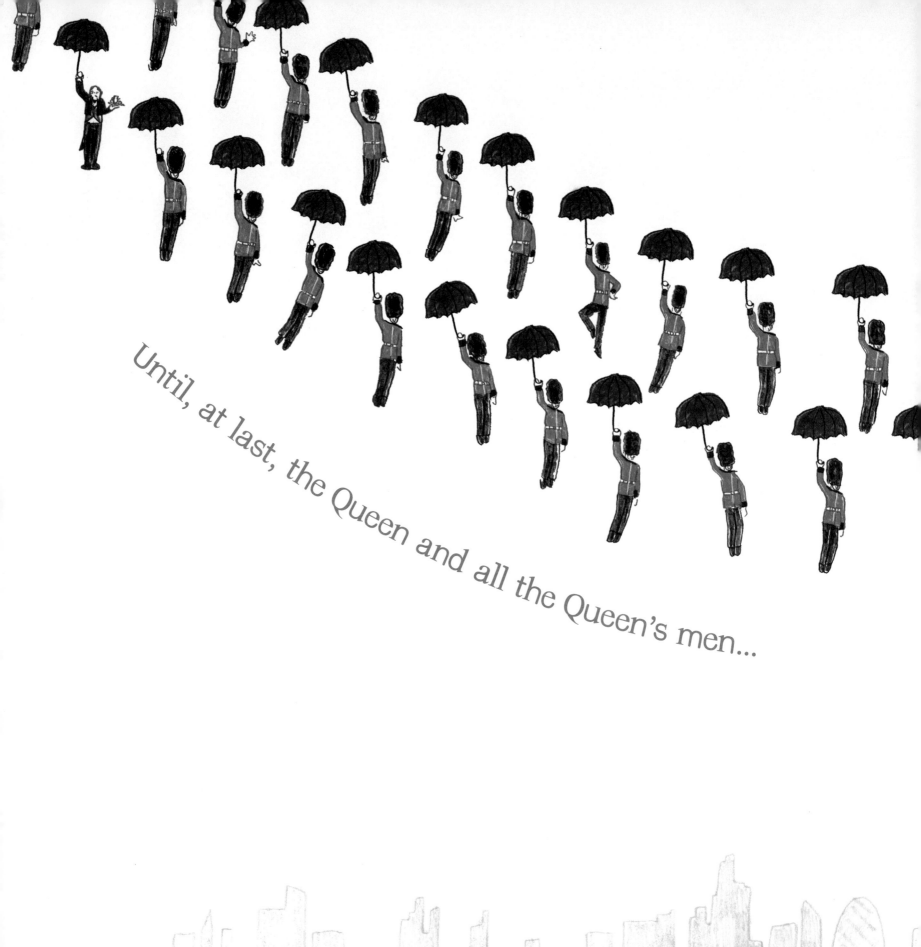

Until, at last, the Queen and all the Queen's men...

floated gently down...

to Kensington Palace...

along with the Queen's...

...hat!